Type set in Korinna
The art was done in oil paints
Design by Filomena Tuosto

Published by Bloomsbury, New York and London
Distributed to the trade by Holtzbrinck Publishers
Library of Congress Cataloging-in-Publication Data
available upon request

First U.S. Edition
1 3 5 7 9 10 8 6 4 2

Bloomsbury USA Children's Books
175 Fifth Avenue
New York, New York 10010

All papers used by Bloomsbury Publishing are natural, recyclable products
made from wood grown in sustainable, well-managed forests.  The manufacturing
processes conform to the environmental regulations of the country of origin.

This book is dedicated in loving memory to

*Dorothy and Gertrude Lathrop*

**O**nce upon a time in a beautiful blue house bordering the woods lived two artists who were sisters. Outside this house, in the woods, lived a large family of mice. The youngest and most adventuresome was Lucy. She had heard about the sisters, how they worked all day making beautiful things, and how they loved animals. Lucy decided *this* was where she wanted to live.

But no mouse had ever tried to live permanently in the big house.

The sisters carried Lucy in a safe trap back to her old home in the woods. Dorothy, the taller and older sister, fed her sunflower seeds. Gertrude told her, "This is where you belong, free in the woods. Now don't you come back!"

Lucy didn't understand a word they said. She thanked them for bringing her out to visit her family.
"Squeak! Squeak!"

The next time Lucy went back to the house she brought friends with her. The mice had fun watching Gertrude make clay sculptures of animal models. They liked to be models too!

At night, Lucy and her friends slid down the sculptures in the quiet moonlit studio.

During the day they napped on the shelves in Dorothy's studio. It seemed to the mice that the sisters were going to let them stay.

One day Lucy and her friends smelled Dorothy's special sugar lace cookies baking. The mice woke up and ate cookies right off the cooling rack!

The sisters didn't like this one bit. They caught the mice and carried them back to the woods. They told the mice, "Now don't you come back!"

Lucy and her friends ran off to tell their families about the sugar lace cookies.

The word was out. Sugar lace cookies. And *all* the mice wanted to taste them!

By now the sisters were tired of sending the mice away. Gertrude welcomed them with matchbox beds lined with soft flannel.

Dorothy gave them their own plate of sugar lace cookies. Lucy and her friends happily posed for the stories Dorothy wrote about them.

These books about mice were so lovingly told that even households that were not mouse-friendly became devoted mouse fans.

One of those stories was about two women who
learned to live with mice. These mice, including one
in particular named Lucy, lived happily ever after,
eating sugar lace cookies and dreaming sweet dreams
in a beautiful blue house bordering the woods.

# A Note From the Author

*Dorothy Lathrop was a famous author and illustrator of children's books who was the first recipient of the Caldecott Medal in 1938.*

*Gertrude Lathrop, her sister, was a renowned sculptor who knew many political figures of her time, including Eleanor Roosevelt.*

*Both artists were early advocates for animals.*

*When I was a teenager I had the honor to meet and garden for the sisters who were then in their eighties. We were kindred spirits in our love of art and of the animals.*